The Adventures of Jim-Bob
A BEARography

Sleep tight little ones !

Krista D. Earp-Bridgmon, PhD
with Illustrations by Emily Inman, PsyD

Abbott Press books may be ordered through booksellers or by contacting:

Abbott Press
1663 Liberty Drive
Bloomington, IN 47403
www.abbottpress.com
Phone: 1-866-697-5310

Because of the dynamic nature of the Internet, any web addresses or links contained in this book may have changed since publication and may no longer be valid. The views expressed in this work are solely those of the author and do not necessarily reflect the views of the publisher, and the publisher hereby disclaims any responsibility for them.

Any people depicted in stock imagery provided by Thinkstock are models, and such images are being used for illustrative purposes only.

Certain stock imagery © Thinkstock.

ISBN: 978-1-4582-1005-0 (sc)
ISBN: 978-1-4582-1004-3 (e)

Library of Congress Control Number: 2013911002

Printed in the United States of America.

Abbott Press rev. date: 7/16/2013

abbott press
A DIVISION OF WRITER'S DIGEST

Dedication:

This book is dedicated to Julie for inspiring and bringing Jim-Bob to so many lives across the world and to Coltin for inspiring me every day in every way that is good. I love you.

Acknowledgements:

I would like to thank the following individuals for their feedback and suggestions with this project.

Christopher Messer, Ph.D., Sociology Professor

Kaeley Nepplova, B.S., Secondary Language Arts Teacher

Carrie Quinn, M.Ed., Elementary Teacher

Pamela Richmond, Ph.D., Social Work Professor

Karen Yescavage, Ph.D., Social Psychology Professor

This is a story about a teddy bear named Jim-Bob. One Saturday, Jim-Bob started his morning reading a new book. The book was about all the different places in the world. Jim-Bob remembered learning of these places from school when his teacher told the class about different continents on the Planet Earth. Since Jim-Bob had only lived in his house, he wondered who lived on these continents. He then decided to set out on an adventure to meet some new friends and see these new lands.

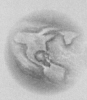

Jim-Bob started his travels in North America where he met a grizzly bear named Gus. Gus was quite a bit larger than Jim-Bob, but they had the same color of brown fur. At first, Jim-Bob was a little frightened of Gus because he was so big and made loud noises.

Jim-Bob watched Gus dig a hole for a few minutes and soon asked, "What are you doing digging that big hole?" Gus replied, "This is where I live, my home is called a den. I made it myself. This is where I rest and spend time with my family." Jim-Bob was very excited to learn where Gus lived and quickly shared that he had a home too, but it looked a little different. Jim-Bob shared with Gus that his home had a bed with blankets, but he also goes there after school to spend time with family.

Jim-Bob's second stop was to South America. It was there he met a Spectacled Bear named Sam. Sam had beautiful black fur with little spots of white on her chest that looked like freckles. Sam didn't see Jim-Bob at first because she had climbed the highest tree and was up there eating some fruit.

When Jim-Bob spotted Sam, he quickly asked, "What are you doing up so high in that tree?" Sam replied, "I like to climb as high as I can to see the beautiful land of South America. This is my home and I really like it." Jim-Bob was very excited to learn where Sam lived and quickly told her about the huge tree that was in his back yard. He said, "Sometimes I go in my tree house at my home too. It's really high and beautiful. I guess we both really like where we live because it is nice with pretty things to see."

Jim-Bob traveled to his continent, Antarctica. It was very cold and there was snow in every direction he looked. He was happy he had on his sweater. Because everything was white with snow, he almost didn't see Paul the Polar Bear because he blended in with his white fur. Paul too was on vacation from the Arctic visiting the beautiful southern continent.

When Paul saw Jim-Bob he asked if he wanted to play. Jim-Bob didn't know what sort of games polar bears like to take part in, but said he would like to play. "Do you want to play hide and go seek?", Jim-Bob asked. Jim-Bob thought that would be a fun game because Paul would be difficult to find when it was Jim-Bob's turn to seek. Paul responded, "I want to go swimming." Jim-Bob had never learned to swim, but Paul said he would teach him. Since Jim-Bob loved learning and was a good listener, he soon was swimming well. After the swim, Jim-Bob thanked Paul for teaching him a new skill. Jim-Bob then taught Paul how to play hide and go seek. Just as Jim-Bob predicted, Paul was very good at hiding. They had a great time together. After taking turns hiding and seeking, Jim-Bob was ready to set out for his next adventure.

Jim-Bob traveled north from Antarctica to Africa where he was immediately greeted by an Atlas bear named Amara. When Jim-Bob first saw Amara, he thought she looked gloomy. As he approached her he asked, "You look like you feel sad, is there something I can do to help you feel better?" Amara thanked Jim-Bob for his concern. She replied that she felt lonely. Amara was on her way to climb the Atlas Mountains to seek more Atlas bears like her to play. Jim-Bob told her that sometimes he feels lonely too and that he would help her. They traveled up the mountain together as a team. On the way up the mountain, Jim-Bob told Amara that when he feels lonely, he asks a classmate if they would like to play at recess or work on a puzzle together.

As they approached the top of the mountain, Amara was able to find more Atlas bears. Amara's friends shared with Jim-Bob stories of Africa and what Amara was like when she was just an Atlas bear cub. Jim-Bob shared in return stories of his home and what he was like when he was just a teddy bear cub. Jim-Bob thanked Amara for the enjoyable journey and the time they spent together. He left and was on his way back down the mountain for his next quest.

Jim-Bob used his compass to travel north to Europe. He was surprised how different this land was from his previous destinations. He was drawn to a large, green, grassy area just at the bottom of another mountain. Jim-Bob thought since Amara liked to climb mountains, maybe other bears like mountains too. As he approached this climb, he noticed a big brown bear running very fast in the field. Jim-Bob was worried there was danger nearby and finally was able to stop the bear to ask why he was running so fast.

"Hi there little bear! My name is Baldo and I like to run fast, there is no danger little bear so you don't need to be scared." Jim-Bob felt relief and started asking the brown bear questions. "I always stand on two legs, but when you were running, you were using all four of your legs. I can teach you to stand on two legs. Can you teach me how to run fast on four legs?" Jim-Bob asked. Baldo said he would love to teach Jim-Bob how to run fast. At first, Jim-Bob ran slowly with four legs, but after some practice, he too was running very fast just like Baldo. Jim-Bob was so proud of himself that he learned to run swiftly. And just as it took some practice to run on four legs, it took Baldo several attempts, but he was able to stand on two legs. Baldo couldn't wait to share with his friends this new trick and Jim-Bob couldn't wait to run fast again. So he quickly ran east through the field waving good-bye to Baldo, his new friend.

Jim-Bob ran a long distance before finding himself among many trees in a continent called Asia. There were so many long, green trees, Jim-Bob couldn't even see the sky any longer. Just then, Jim-Bob saw a large animal sitting under one of the biggest trees there. The animal had black and white fur and appeared to be eating something. As Jim-Bob went to meet him, he noticed his tummy growling. He wondered if the black and white animal would share some of his snack.

"Hi! My name is Jim-Bob. What is your name?" Jim-Bob asked. "My name is Ping," said the Giant Panda. "It's nice to meet you Ping. I've been running, traveling, and experiencing new lands for quite some time. Would you mind sharing your snack with me?" Jim-Bob requested. "Here, try this bamboo. It's the best in the forest." Jim-Bob didn't know you could eat trees, but it did look tasty and it was! While snacking, Jim-Bob told Ping about the snacks he eats at home. Jim-Bob's favorite snacks were cheese, Vanilla Wafers and Goldfish Crackers.

Ping gave Jim-Bob some more bamboo to munch on while he finished his travels. Jim-Bob was very thankful to Ping for showing him a new tasty treat and started south to the next adventure.

For Jim-Bob's last voyage, he visited a place others called, "Down Under". He didn't understand this phrase so he decided to travel south to take a look and make some observations. It was a quiet land also with many, many trees. All of the sudden, he heard a loud snore. Jim-Bob looked up and there he saw a small animal sleeping in the tree.

Jim-Bob tried really hard to remain quiet as he didn't want to wake the snoring creature, but he stepped on a tree branch which woke the koala. "Hey there little teddy bear, can I help you find something?", said the koala. "I'm looking for a land called, 'Down Under'. Am I there?" The koala replied, "Yes, this continent is called Australia and it's where I live. My name is Kody. What is your name?"

Jim-Bob responded by telling the koala his name, but looked puzzled. "What's wrong?" asked Kody. Jim-Bob responded, "I'm a teddy bear, but I'm not sure what type of bear you are." Kody responded, "I'm not a bear, I'm a marsupial, but I get called a bear all the time. Thank you for asking me. What brings you to Australia?"

Jim-Bob shared his adventure with Kody. "Well, I learned how to dig a hole called a den in North America by a grizzly bear named Gus. I learned how to climb a tall tree in South America by a speckled bear named Sam. I learned how to swim the cold water in Antarctica by a polar bear named Paul. I learned how to climb a mountain in Africa by an Atlas bear named Amara. I learned how to run really fast in Europe by a brown bear named Baldo. I learned how to eat bamboo in Asia by a Giant Panda named Ping. Now, I'm tired!"

Kody replied, "That sounds like a great adventure where you learned something new and exciting from each new friend. I too can teach you how to do something as your adventure comes to an end." "What is it?" Jim-Bob asked. "SLEEP!" said Kody. "Koalas like to sleep and it sounds like you could use some rest."

Jim-Bob agreed as his eyes quickly fell shut. "That sounds like a great idea Kody. I also like to sleep," Jim-Bob said sleepily and they snored the rest of the day away.

CPSIA information can be obtained
at www.ICGtesting.com
Printed in the USA
LVIC03n0005300713
345247LV00003B

9 781458 210050